For Khéops —X.D.

Copyright © 2004 by NordSüd Verlag AG, Gossau Zürich, Switzerland
First published in Switzerland under the title ICH HAB DICH SO VERMISST!
English translation copyright © 2006 by North-South Books Inc., New York.

All rights reserved. No part of this book may be reproduced or utilized in any form or by any means,
electronic or mechanical, including photocopying, recording, or any information storage and retrieval system,
without permission in writing from the publisher.

First published in the United States, Great Britain, Canada, Australia, and New Zealand in 2006 by North-South Books Inc.,
an imprint of NordSüd Verlag AG, Gossau Zürich, Switzerland. Distributed in the United States by North-South Books Inc., New York.

Library of Congress Cataloging-in-Publication Data is available.
A CIP catalogue record for this book is available from The British Library.

ISBN-13: 978-0-7358-2003-6 / ISBN-10: 0-7358-2003-1 (trade edition)
10 9 8 7 6 5 4 3 2 1

Printed in Belgium

Friends
for All Seasons

By Géraldine Elschner

Concept and Illustrations by

Xavière Devos

Translated by Marianne Martens

NORTHSOUTH
BOOKS

New York · London

Bright and early one morning a sharp whistle rang through the forest. Sunny jumped out of bed. "I'm coming!" she cried. She knew exactly who was calling to her.

It was Milly the little marmot.
Sunny quickly slid down the tree, and soon the two best friends were
running across the meadow. After a few somersaults, Milly pulled five
pinecones out of her pocket and they worked on their juggling routine,
tossing the cones back and forth, faster and faster.

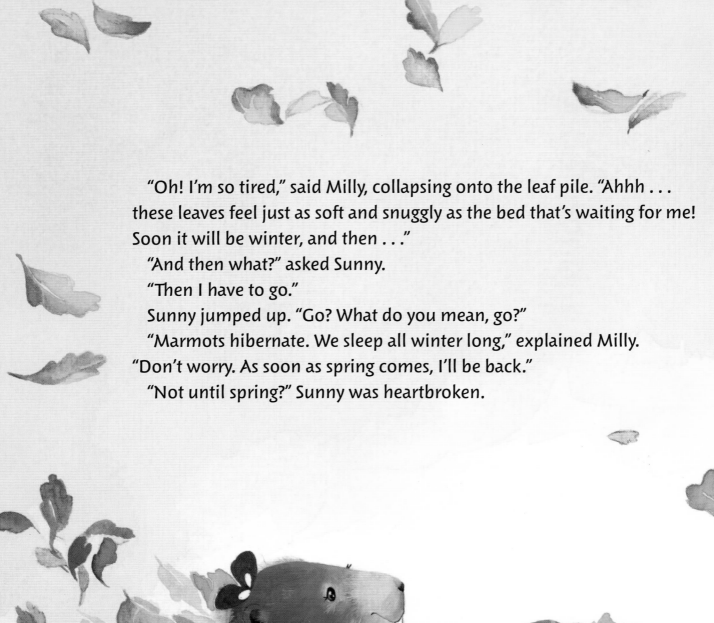

"Oh! I'm so tired," said Milly, collapsing onto the leaf pile. "Ahhh . . . these leaves feel just as soft and snuggly as the bed that's waiting for me! Soon it will be winter, and then . . ."

"And then what?" asked Sunny.

"Then I have to go."

Sunny jumped up. "Go? What do you mean, go?"

"Marmots hibernate. We sleep all winter long," explained Milly. "Don't worry. As soon as spring comes, I'll be back."

"Not until spring?" Sunny was heartbroken.

As the weeks passed, Milly got sleepier and sleepier, and one day . . .
"I can hardly keep my eyes open," she said. "Now it's time for me to go."
"I'm going to miss you so much," whispered Sunny sadly.

"I'll miss you too, but I'll play with you in my dreams! Take good care of our pinecones and think of me when you juggle."
They hugged, and Milly scurried off.

Sunny couldn't fall asleep that night.

The whole winter without her best friend! How could she stand it?

Mama tried to comfort her. "You can play with your brothers and your other forest friends," she suggested.

"I know," said Sunny with a sigh.

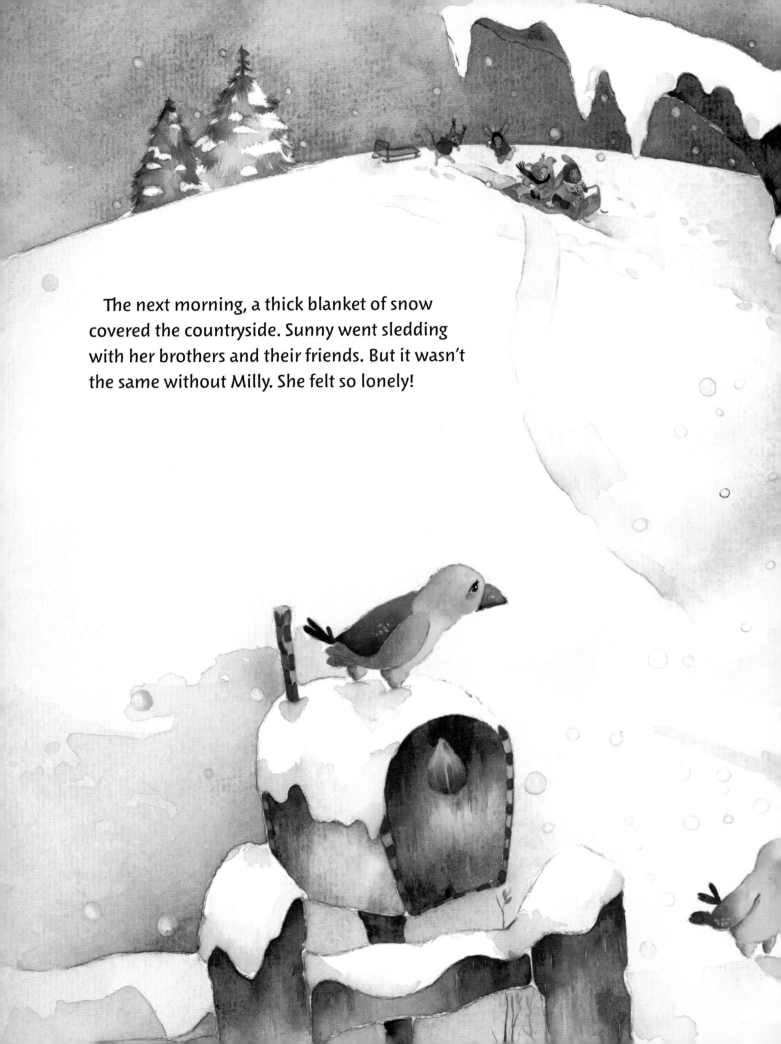

The next morning, a thick blanket of snow covered the countryside. Sunny went sledding with her brothers and their friends. But it wasn't the same without Milly. She felt so lonely!

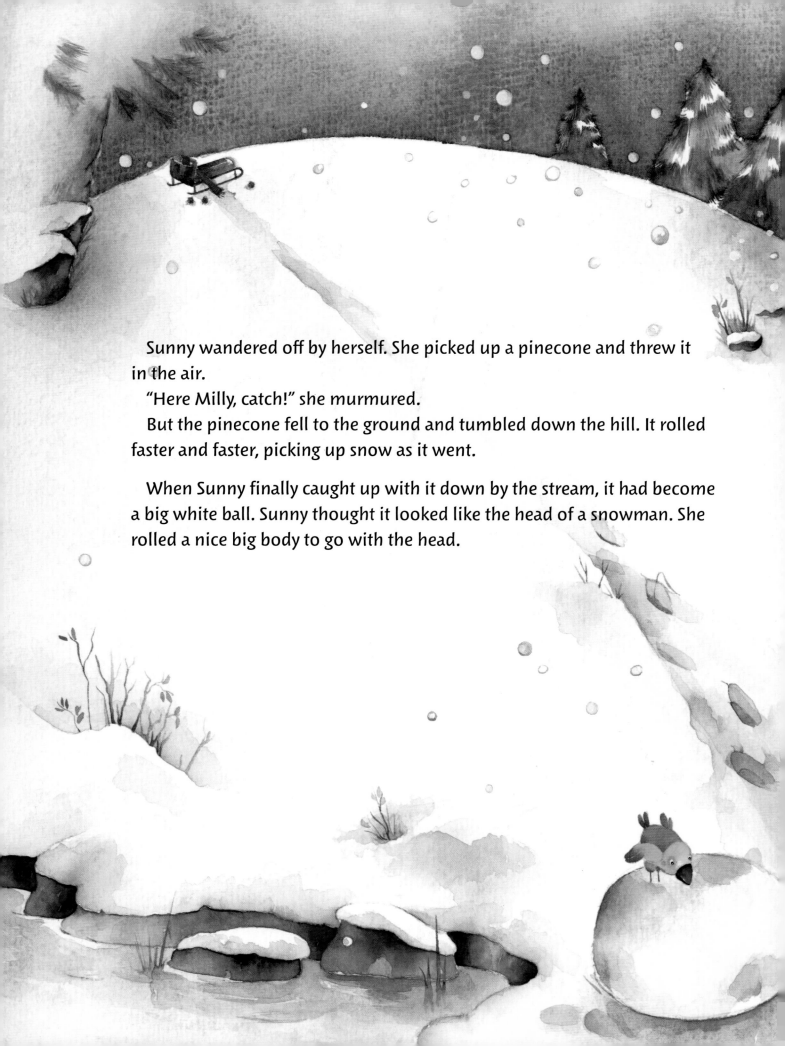

Sunny wandered off by herself. She picked up a pinecone and threw it in the air.

"Here Milly, catch!" she murmured.

But the pinecone fell to the ground and tumbled down the hill. It rolled faster and faster, picking up snow as it went.

When Sunny finally caught up with it down by the stream, it had become a big white ball. Sunny thought it looked like the head of a snowman. She rolled a nice big body to go with the head.

"One more branch, and you're done!" said Sunny.

"Thanks a lot!" said a friendly voice.

Sunny nearly jumped out of her fur. "What? You can talk?"

"Of course I can, and sing too! My name is Fred, and I like anything red!" sang the snowman.

"My name is Sunny, and I like songs that are funny!" giggled Sunny.

From then on, Sunny visited her snowman every day. And every day, she brought him new surprises. Fred was always in a good mood. Together, they made up rhymes, songs, and jokes. Fred told the most wonderful stories.

Sunny told Fred all about her friend Milly. And whenever she played Milly's special song on her flute, Fred and the birds would sing along.

"Look! The first spring flowers are here!" said Fred one day. "Your friend will wake up soon. And I'll have to go."

Sunny jumped up. "Go? What do you mean go?"

"All snowmen melt in the warm spring sun. Soon I'll melt into the stream, and tumble down into the valley."

Sunny had tears in her eyes.

"Don't worry," said Fred. "I'll be back next winter when it snows again."

A few days later, Sunny went to the stream. In the middle of a puddle, she saw a branch, a pinecone, her soggy scarf, and an old hat. Sunny sat under the tree and cried. How she missed Fred!

Then suddenly . . .

. . . a loud whistle rang through the forest.

"Milly! Finally!" cried Sunny, and gave
Milly a big hug.

"How was your winter?" asked Milly.

Sunny told her friend all about Fred the
snowman.

"A snowman? I've never seen anything like
that." Milly was amazed.

"Oh, he was wonderful!" said Sunny. "And he had
wonderful stories, too. I'll tell them to you and it
will be almost as good as if you'd been there. And
next winter when he returns, he'll have new jokes
and stories."

And so, as they headed off to play, they planned
all the wonderful things they would do together
through the spring and summer and autumn. . . .